The North Wind and the Sun

'14

'020

?20

A traditional tale

First published in 2004 by
Franklin Watts
96 Leonard Street
London
EC2A 4XD

Franklin Watts Australia
45–51 Huntley Street
Alexandria
NSW 2015

Text © Margaret Nash 2004
Illustration © Kate Sheppard 2004

A CIP catalogue record for this book is available
from the British Library.

ISBN 0 7496 5744 8 (hbk)
ISBN 0 7496 5782 0 (pbk)

Series Editor: Jackie Hamley
Series Advisors: Dr Barrie Wade, Dr Hilary Minns
Design: Peter Scoulding

Printed in Hong Kong / China

To Daniel, with love – MN

Notes for parents and teachers

READING CORNER has been structured to provide maximum support for new readers. The stories may be used by adults for sharing with young children. Primarily, however, the stories are designed for newly independent readers, whether they are reading these books in bed at night, or in the reading corner at school or in the library.

Starting to read alone can be a daunting prospect. READING CORNER helps by providing visual support and repeating words and phrases, while making reading enjoyable. These books will develop confidence in the new reader, and encourage a love of reading that will last a lifetime!

If you are reading this book with a child, here are a few tips:

1. Make reading fun! Choose a time to read when you and the child are relaxed and have time to share the story.

2. Encourage children to reread the story, and to retell the story in their own words, using the illustrations to remind them what has happened.

3. Give praise! Remember that small mistakes need not always be corrected.

READING CORNER covers three grades of early reading ability, with three levels at each grade. Each level has a certain number of words per story, indicated by the number of bars on the spine of the book, to allow you to choose the right book for a young reader:

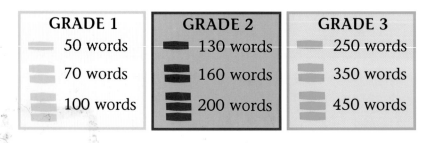

GRADE 1	GRADE 2	GRADE 3
50 words	130 words	250 words
70 words	160 words	350 words
100 words	200 words	450 words

The North Wind and the Sun

Retold by
Margaret Nash

Illustrated by
Kate Sheppard

W
FRANKLIN WATTS
LONDON•SYDNEY

Margaret Nash

"I love to hear the wind rustling through the trees in my garden. I also love to see the sun shining through them!"

Kate Sheppard

"I love to feel the wind on my face and the sun on my back when I walk by the sea. I hope you enjoy the book!"

One day, the North Wind
met the Sun.

"I'm stronger than you!"
said the Wind.

"Do you think so?" said the Sun.

9

The Wind puffed himself up until he was very fat: PUFF PUFF PUFF!

11

" I bet I can get the coat off
that man," said the Wind.

"Very well," said the Sun, and he sat on a cloud to watch.

PUFF PUFF PUFF! The Wind
puffed until he almost burst.

But the man just pulled his
coat around him tighter.

"Now let me try," said the Sun.

He shone as hard as he could.

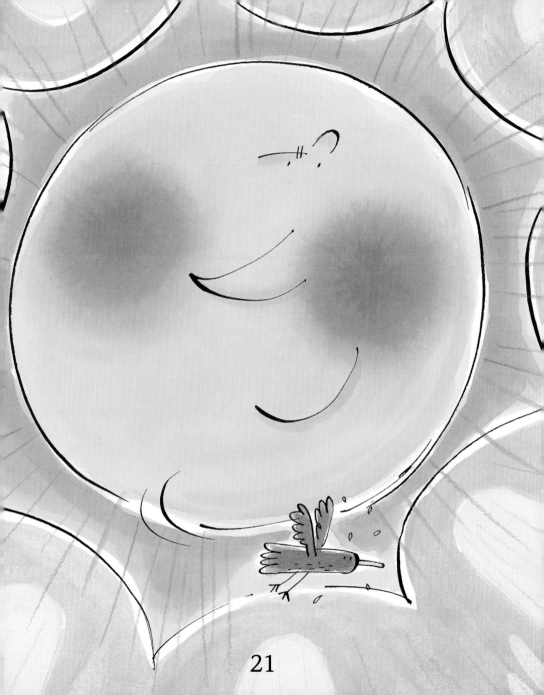

21

It got warm ...

... then hot ...

... then hotter!

"Phew!" said the man.
He had a drink
and then ...

... he threw off his coat!

"Wow!" said the Wind.
"You did it!"

"Yes," said the Sun, and he smiled the biggest smile he'd ever smiled.

Notes for parents and teachers

READING CORNER has been structured to provide maximum support for new readers. The stories may be used by adults for sharing with young children. Primarily, however, the stories are designed for newly independent readers, whether they are reading these books in bed at night, or in the reading corner at school or in the library.

Starting to read alone can be a daunting prospect. READING CORNER helps by providing visual support and repeating words and phrases, while making reading enjoyable. These books will develop confidence in the new reader, and encourage a love of reading that will last a lifetime!

If you are reading this book with a child, here are a few tips:

1. Make reading fun! Choose a time to read when you and the child are relaxed and have time to share the story.

2. Encourage children to reread the story, and to retell the story in their own words, using the illustrations to remind them what has happened.

3. Give praise! Remember that small mistakes need not always be corrected.

READING CORNER covers three grades of early reading ability, with three levels at each grade. Each level has a certain number of words per story, indicated by the number of bars on the spine of the book, to allow you to choose the right book for a young reader:

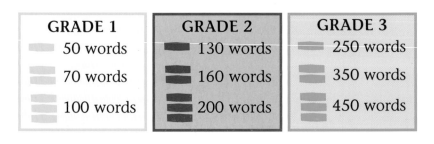

GRADE 1	GRADE 2	GRADE 3
50 words	130 words	250 words
70 words	160 words	350 words
100 words	200 words	450 words